CH00573489

margaret Tempest.

LITTLE GREY RABBIT
MAKES LACE

Little Grey Rabbit Books

SQUIRREL GOES SKATING
WISE OWL'S STORY
LITTLE GREY RABBIT'S PARTY
THE KNOT SQUIRREL TIED
FUZZYPEG GOES TO SCHOOL
LITTLE GREY RABBIT'S CHRISTMAS
MOLDY WARP THE MOLE
HARE JOINS THE HOME GUARD
LITTLE GREY RABBIT'S WASHING DAY
WATER RAT'S PICNIC
LITTLE GREY RABBIT'S BIRTHDAY
THE SPECKLEDY HEN
LITTLE GREY RABBIT TO THE RESCUE (*Play*)
LITTLE GREY RABBIT AND THE WEASELS
GREY RABBIT AND THE WANDERING HEDGEHOG
LITTLE GREY RABBIT MAKES LACE
HARE AND THE EASTER EGGS
LITTLE GREY RABBIT'S VALENTINE
LITTLE GREY RABBIT GOES TO THE SEA
HARE AND GUY FAWKES
LITTLE GREY RABBIT'S PAINT BOX
GREY RABBIT FINDS A SHOE
GREY RABBIT AND THE CIRCUS
GREY RABBIT'S MAY DAY
HARE GOES SHOPPING
LITTLE GREY RABBIT'S PANCAKE DAY

Illustrated by Katherine Wigglesworth
LITTLE GREY RABBIT GOES TO THE NORTH POLE
FUZZYPEG'S BROTHER
LITTLE GREY RABBIT'S SPRING CLEANING PARTY
LITTLE GREY RABBIT AND THE SNOW BABY

Little Grey Rabbit
Makes Lace

by Alison Uttley
Pictures by
Margaret Tempest

Collins London

FIRST PUBLISHED 1950
THIRTEENTH IMPRESSION 1983

ISBN 0 00 194116 X

COPYRIGHT RESERVED
PRINTED IN GREAT BRITAIN
WILLIAM COLLINS SONS & CO LTD GLASGOW

FOREWORD

OF course you must understand that Grey Rabbit's home had no electric light or gas, and even the candles were made from pith of rushes dipped in wax from the wild bees' nests, which Squirrel found. Water there was in plenty, but it did not come from a tap. It flowed from a spring outside, which rose up from the ground and went to a brook. Grey Rabbit cooked on a fire, but it was a wood fire, there was no coal in that part of the country. Tea did not come from India, but from a little herb known very well to country people, who once dried it and used it in their cottage homes. Bread was baked from wheat ears, ground fine, and Hare and Grey Rabbit gleaned in the cornfields to get the wheat.

The doormats were plaited rushes, like country-made mats, and cushions were stuffed with wool gathered from the hedges where sheep pushed through the thorns. As for the looking-glass, Grey Rabbit found the glass, dropped from a lady's handbag, and Mole made a frame for it. Usually the animals gazed at themselves in the still pools as so many country children have done. The country ways of Grey Rabbit were the country ways known to the author.

GREY RABBIT sat at her cottage
door one fine morning with her
work-basket at her side and the scissors
on the doorstep. She was making a
night-cap for Mrs. Hedgehog out of a
little pink handkerchief. Hare had
picked it up on the common, dropped
from somebody's pocket. Grey Rabbit
decided it was just right for a night-
cap. She snipped the edge neatly and
sewed a hem, shaping it to fit Mrs.
Hedgehog's head. Her little needle
flew in and out of the linen and her
stitches were so small they were almost
invisible.

"THIS will keep Mrs. Hedgehog warm at night when she peeps through the window at the moon," thought the busy rabbit. "She got a cold, moon-gazing last month, poor Mrs. Hedgehog. It was clever of Hare to find this piece of linen. He is really a remarkable Hare."

It was very quiet in the cottage, for Hare and Squirrel had gone out together across the fields to visit the Speckledy Hen, but in the trees all the birds were singing. Grey Rabbit could hear a blackbird playing his little flute, and a tom-tit ringing a peal of bells. A speckled thrush was calling.

"I SEE YOU. I SEE YOU. Kiss me. Kiss me." And a green woodpecker laughed loudly.

There was a flutter of wings and Robin the postman flew down with his letter-bag, from which he took a little green-leaf letter.

"You're lucky to-day, Grey Rabbit. Here's a letter."

"A letter for me?" cried Grey Rabbit, dropping her sewing.

"It's not very important. I read it first," said the Robin. "I should have come at once if it had been URGENT but it's nothing much. So I stopped to weed my garden first."

9

"DEAR ROBIN," laughed Grey
Rabbit. " I can't even read it, it
has such crooked letters."

" It says : ' Riddle-me-ree,
           I'm coming to tea,' "
said the postman. " Never a please or
thank you, or anything."

" Who sent it? " asked Grey
Rabbit, turning it over and looking at
the back.   Then she saw the letter
F scribbled on the stalk.

" Ah! It's from Fuzzypeg," she
cried. " He knows he is always wel-
come."

I MIGHT HAVE GUESSED! I saw the little hedgehog go past with his schoolbag early this morning. I'll say good-bye, now, Grey Rabbit, and go back to my garden."

The Robin flew away with his empty postbag flapping behind him, and Grey Rabbit took up her sewing. The needle had fallen out, and she hunted in the grass for it.

"Cuckoo! Cuckoo!" cried a small squeaky voice, and there stood Fuzzy-peg with his pointed nose pushed between the bars of the gate.

"Cuckoo! Did you think it was the Cuckoo, Grey Rabbit?" he asked, hopefully.

"WELL, A PRICKLY CUCKOO with no wings," said Grey Rabbit, running to let him in. "Come along, little Fuzzypeg. I've just had a nice letter from you. I am so glad you've come."

"I thought I would and I did," said Fuzzypeg. "It was a holiday, and I didn't know, so I've been finding presents all day."

He slipped his paw in his left pocket and brought out a robin's pin-cushion. "It's the reddest pin-cushion I've ever seen on a rose-bush. It's for you to stick your pins in, Grey Rabbit."

LITTLE GREY RABBIT thanked him and put it in her work-basket, but Fuzzypeg dived deep into his right pocket and brought out a double-daisy. Then he went to his left pocket for a peacock butterfly, and to his right for a ladybird in a spotted cloak. Finally from the left pocket came a green shining beetle.

"Oh, thank you, Fuzzypeg," said Grey Rabbit, as all these things appeared. The butterfly flew on the work-box and sunned its wings. The ladybird settled on the pink linen cap. The little emerald beetle walked straight to the needle and stood by it.

"OH, LOOK! He's found my lost needle," cried Grey Rabbit. "Isn't he clever!"

"I thought he was a special beetle," agreed Fuzzypeg. "That's why I brought him to see you."

He ran indoors and fetched a stool and sat down by his friend's side. He watched Grey Rabbit thread her needle and make her tiny stitches.

"What are you making, Grey Rabbit?" he asked.

"Hush! It's for your mother," she whispered. "It's a night-cap."

"She *will* be pleased, Grey Rabbit." Fuzzypeg stroked the soft linen admiringly. "She made a wish for a night-cap."

"GREY RABBIT," he continued, "I've seen something to-day."

"Yes? What is it?" Grey Rabbit smiled at the eager face turned towards her.

"I went across the common early this morning, to post your letter, and do you know, there was lace hanging on the gorse."

"Lace? What kind of lace?"

"Very nice lace, silver and grey, all dangling from the prickles. Where did it come from, Grey Rabbit?"

"I expect it was the spiders' weaving. They are clever creatures, Fuzzypeg. They hang out their silver webs in the bushes to catch sunbeams."

" I TRIED to bring you some, but it all curled up to nothing," said Fuzzypeg.

" You can't carry it, Fuzzypeg dear."

" I think my mother would like some lace on her cap. Can you make it, Grey Rabbit? You can do most things," said the little Hedgehog.

" I can't make lace," sighed Grey Rabbit. " I'll ask Squirrel when she comes home. I can hear voices in the fields now. Squirrel and Hare will soon be here."

Riddle-me-ree, I want my tea," sang Fuzzypeg, leaping up, and he and Grey Rabbit ran indoors to set the table.

FUZZYPEG toasted the muffins, and Grey Rabbit washed the lettuces and radishes, and put them on the little plates. She brought a cake from the larder and a loaf of currant bread from the bread-mug. There was a pat of butter, a jug of milk and a bowl of nuts. She was just making the tea when the garden gate rattled and Squirrel and Hare came racing up the path into the house. Fuzzypeg hid under the table. He suddenly felt shy.

" Is tea ready, Grey Rabbit? We are hungry! " cried Squirrel, tossing a bunch of flowers on the table.

"GREY RABBIT! Grey Rabbit!" shouted Hare. "We saw Speckledy Hen and she sent two eggs for your tea. I rolled one down a hill, and it went so fast I couldn't catch it."

"Not till it was broken," explained Squirrel. "Then we caught it, after it had bounced."

"Then we licked it up," added Hare.

"And where's the other egg?" asked Grey Rabbit.

"Well, we tried to see if it could swim," said Hare.

"And did it?"

"No, it was drowned in the stream among the forget-me-nots. Poor little egg," said Hare sadly.

"POOR LITTLE EGG," echoed Grey Rabbit, and a tiny whimper came from under the table, but just then Hare noticed the little pink cap lying neatly folded on the work-basket. He snatched it up and set it on his long ears.

Then he danced round singing :
"A hunting-cap for me.
A hunting-cap for me.
I'll catch the wicked Fox
And put him in a box,
And serve him up for tea."

"NO, IT'S FOR ME," cried Squirrel, grabbing the cap from Hare and perching it on her own red head, singing :

"A hunting-cap for me.
A hunting-cap for me.
I'll catch the little Weasel,
And beat him with a Teazel,
And never set him free."

"It isn't for either of you," shrieked an indignant, muffled voice, and Fuzzypeg scrambled out and pulled Squirrel's tail. "It's for my mother." He was half-crying.

"HALLO, FUZZYPEG! What are you doing here?" cried Hare.

"I've come for tea, and it's a hunting-cap for my mother, it is," sobbed Fuzzypeg.

"It's a night-cap for Mrs. Hedgehog, made out of the handkerchief you found, Hare," explained Grey Rabbit. "It's to keep her warm when she looks at the new moon."

"My mother always makes a c-c-c-c-curtsey to-o th-the n-n-new m-m-moon and she gets a w-w-wish," sobbed Fuzzypeg. "She w-w-wished for a hunt-hunt-night-cap and th-this is it."

"NOW COME ALONG and have tea, all of you," said Grey Rabbit. "Fuzzypeg must have the biggest muffin, and the slice of cake with cherries on the top."

"Dry your eyes, Fuzzypeg, and sit by me," she continued, and Fuzzypeg rubbed his face in his smock and sat close to Grey Rabbit.

"Squirrel, can you make lace?" asked Fuzzypeg suddenly cheerful, as he gobbled up his muffin.

"No, I can't, but I know where Queen Anne's Lace grows," answered Squirrel.

"Queen Anne's Lace? What's that?" Fuzzypeg stared at Squirrel.

"IT'S THE FOAMY WHITE FLOWER that fills the hedgebanks and ditches, where you hide when anyone goes past," said Hare.

"Oh, yes. I know it. I've often hidden in it."

"I once made a boot-lace," said Hare. "It was a very good one, made from a green rush, and I threaded it through a boot. What do you want lace for, Fuzzypeg? Would a boot-lace do?"

"It's for my mother's night-cap, to go round the edge," said Fuzzypeg.

GREY RABBIT explained about the gossamer lace which hung on the hedges and gorse-bushes. They all shook their heads, saying nobody could make lace except the spiders and perhaps the field-mice. The mice had sharp teeth, they could surely make lace.

" I'll go to-morrow to visit the field-mice and the spiders, Fuzzypeg, and when I have some lace I will trim the cap ready for the new moon."

" Yes, and when my mother makes her wish, I'll pop it on her head. Won't she be surprised! " laughed Fuzzypeg, clapping his hands.

WHEN TEA WAS OVER and every scrap on the tiny plates had been eaten, Fuzzypeg ran home.

Grey Rabbit finished sewing the cap, and Squirrel tried it on again.

" It would be lovely with lace round the edge," said she, running to look at herself in the glass.

The next day Grey Rabbit knocked at the door of the little house where the field-mice lived. They invited her to come in, but the house was so small Grey Rabbit thought she would stick fast. Through the open door she could see washing before the fire and a basket of sewing on the table. They were always busy because there were so many children.

"EXCUSE ME, Mrs. Mouse, can you make lace?" asked Grey Rabbit, looking at the frills and little garments hanging there. "You sew so neatly I hope you can make lace."

"Lace, Miss Grey Rabbit? Oh no! We always bite the edges of our frills to make them shaggy, but we cannot weave lace."

SO GREY RABBIT went to the common to ask the spiders about it. They took no notice of her. They were spinning their silken webs and running in and out of the golden gorse flowers, and they had no time for the rabbit.

"I don't think anybody can make lace," said she. So the pink night-cap lay in the work-basket, and the moon grew larger and larger till it was full moon. Then it began to wane, and Grey Rabbit was afraid the new moon would appear like a thin horn in the sky, and Mrs. Hedgehog would have no lace on her cap to greet it.

ONE SUNNY DAY Hare was coming home from a journey, and he took a short cut through the village. It was a bold thing to do, but the children were safe at school, the dogs were asleep, the ducks were busy swimming in the pond, and the cats and babies were curled up in their cradles. Only the blacksmith was tinkling on his hammer and the cobbler was tapping at his shoes.

FROM THE school-room came singing, and Hare listened as he passed the door. He could hear these words chanted by fifty little voices :

" Queen Anne, Queen Anne,
   She sat in the sun,
   Making of lace till the day was done.
   She made it green, she made it white,
   She made it of flowers and sunshine
      and light.
   She fastened it on a stalk so fine,
   She left it in the hedgerow to shine.
   Queen Anne's Lace. Queen Anne's
      Lace.
   You find it growing all over the
      place."

HARE, with ears a-cock and every sense alert, stepped lightly on tip-toe down the street, past the little warm, thatched houses, and the village church and the White Hart Inn. At the door of a pretty cottage, all among roses and lilies, sat an old lady, and there was something about her that made Hare stop still.

For one thing, she smiled at Hare, and her smile was so sweet that Hare felt flattered. He waggled his long ears and smiled back.

FOR ANOTHER THING, she was sitting on a low chair in the porch, with a dark pillow on her lap, and her fingers were moving as swiftly as two darting birds. Hare had never seen human fingers like hers. He was filled with curiosity as he gazed. Little brown wooden bobbins, like toys, with glass beads dangling down, were flying to and fro, and spidery threads were twisting as if a wind blew them.

" She is making music, playing a tune on the pillow," thought Hare, as he listened to the tinkle of the glass beads, and the murmur of the old lady's song as she worked.

"QUEEN ANNE, QUEEN ANNE,
  She sat in the sun,
Making of lace till the day was done."

Then, " Good morning, Mr. Hare,"
she called, nodding her old head in its
sun-bonnet, and tapping with her toes.
Her fingers never stopped flying over
the pillow, twisting the threads, and
then moving some scarlet-headed pins.

" Good morning, Queen Anne," said
Hare politely, remembering the man-
ners Grey Rabbit had taught him, and
he made a little stiff bow.

" Miss Susan," said the old lady.
" That's my name."

" Good morning, Queen Anne,"
repeated Hare, bowing once more.
" Please, what are you doing? "

"WHAT DO YOU think, Mr. Hare?" laughed Miss Susan, whose blue eyes twinkled like two stars.

"I think you are either playing a tune or making Queen Anne's Lace, like the flowers in the hedges," said Hare.

"Clever Hare! I am making lace," said Miss Susan, and her old fingers moved more quickly than ever as she tossed the bobbins about.

Hare leapt up to her, and quite startled her so that she nearly dropped the pillow and all.

"Oh, I am so glad to see you, Queen Anne," said he. "Grey Rabbit wants to make lace. How do you do it?"

"PLEASE DON'T JUMP so wildly, Mr. Hare," said the old lady, as she settled herself again, and arranged the pillow and straightened the threads which hung from the bobbins. "You frightened me. Now watch how I do it."

Hare stood close to her on the door-step, with the lilies and roses waving near. A cart-horse walked slowly up the road, and a man followed towards the smithy where the blacksmith was working, but nobody saw Hare.

HE STARED AT her nimble fingers, following the pattern pricked on a strip of paper laid on her lace-pillow. Every little wooden bobbin was cut in a charming shape, with red, blue and white beads dangling at the ends. The piece of lace with its lovely design lay there, ever growing longer before Hare's eyes.

As she worked the old lady talked to Hare, and told him about lace-making. He told her about Squirrel, Grey Rabbit, Wise Owl, and Moldy Warp, and the cap Grey Rabbit had made for Fuzzypeg's mother. She said it was the nicest tale she had heard for many a long day.

HE WOULD HAVE been there all day if there hadn't been the tinkle-tinkle of a bell in the school-room, and the scamper of little feet in heavy boots, and the laughter of children pouring down the road, free from lessons. They gave a shout when they saw Hare standing by Miss Susan, but Hare saw them in time.

"LOOK! There's a Jack Hare! Catch him! Catch him and put him in a pot. Come on! After him! Let's cook him for dinner."

Hare ran for his life, with his ears laid flat and his big eyes starting with fright.

"Now, children, do 'ee be kind to all of God's creatures," said Miss Susan, dropping the lace-pillow and stepping into the road, but the children raced along and Hare flew in front of them. Dogs and cats, ducks and drakes, cobbler and blacksmith, all joined in the race.

"AND I WON! I won!" cried Hare breathlessly, as he dashed into the cottage and flung himself in the rocking-chair. "They ran and they ran, but they couldn't catch me. I'm the swiftest runner of all. Oh, I'm a wonderful Hare."

"Yes, of course, but where have you been, Hare?" asked Grey Rabbit, as she stooped over the panting animal and wiped his hot face.

"I've been watching Queen Anne make lace, and I can tell you all about it."

"Hare! Hare! Have you really discovered Queen Anne?" cried the delighted Squirrel, bringing Hare a drink of water.

"SHE LIVES in the village and she showed me how to make most beautiful lace. You want a pillow."

"There's a pillow on my bed," said Grey Rabbit, scampering upstairs to fetch it.

"And you want bobbins," continued Hare. "Not cotton-reels, but long bobbins, all carved and made pretty with beads on the ends."

"I'll make them for you," said Rat, pushing his ugly face in at the open door. "I saw Mister Hare running for his life, and I came to help. I'll carve those bobbins for you."

"And I'll get the beads," squeaked Fuzzypeg, peering round after the Rat. "I saw you running, Hare. It was a race."

46

HARE FROWNED and continued his directions.

" You will want a paper pattern with flowers or something pricked on it," said he.

" We'll make the paper pattern, Grey Rabbit, with our sharp teeth. We just came to see why Mister Hare was running so fast."

Hare frowned again as the family of field-mice crowded in the doorway, and he alarmed them so much they retreated to the garden.

" And you will want some fine long threads to make the lace," said he gruffly.

"THERE IS PLENTY of sheep's wool in the hedges," Squirrel cried. " I use it for my knitting, and I can twist fine threads with it."

So the Rat made the lace-bobbins, carved in lovely shapes, some from pieces of bone and some from wood. Fuzzypeg hung beads of hawthorn and berries at the ends for weights.

The field-mice made lace patterns, pricking the paper with rows of bees and flowers. Squirrel wound the wool thread on the bobbins and Hare collected sharp-pointed thorns from the hedges for the lace-pins.

THEN EVERYBODY (except Mrs. Hedgehog, who couldn't understand why the animals were so secretly busy) came to see Grey Rabbit make lace.

The Little Rabbit sat at the door with her pillow on her knee, and the bobbins hanging down. She tossed the bobbins over and crossed the threads and moved the pins down the paper pattern, while they all watched her paws. A tiny strip of lace appeared, and it took the shape of a bee. On she went, and a flower came, and then another bee. She made a row of bees and flowers, with a wavy edge to the sheep's-wool lace like flowing water.

51

THE MICE SQUEAKED in excitement, and Fuzzypeg danced with joy. Hare rushed out to find more wool for Squirrel to twist for the thread, and Rat carved another bobbin. Grey Rabbit's paws, which had moved slowly at first, now flashed backward and forward, and the piece of lace hung down like gossamer.

"I CAN HOLD IT," cried Fuzzypeg. "It doesn't melt away like the spiders' lace."

Then Grey Rabbit sewed it round the night-cap for Mrs. Hedgehog, just in time for the rising of the new moon.

Mrs. Hedgehog went outside to see the moon. She stood in the chilly evening light, and when she saw the lovely pale sickle of the moon in the sky, she solemnly bowed three times. Fuzzypeg, standing by her side, bowed too.

" I WISH FOR A NIGHT-CAP to keep my head warm," murmured Mrs. Hedgehog.

" I wish for some lace round your night-cap," said Fuzzypeg.

Then, from behind his back, he brought out the pink linen night-cap with sheep's-wool lace edging it, and a ribbon bow which Squirrel had kindly provided. He popped it on his mother's head, and how delighted she was !

"I HAVE NEVER SEEN such a lovely cap in all my born days," cried Mrs. Hedgehog, hugging Fuzzy-peg. "Real lace, with bees and flowers all round the edge. It must have been made by a Fairy."

So that is how Grey Rabbit made lace. She trimmed a petticoat for Squirrel and made a cravat for Water-Rat. All the baby rabbits had lace caps. Even Wise Owl got a piece of lace for a keepsake, but he ate it, thinking it was bread and butter.

In the village Miss Susan told a strange story.

"DO YOU MEAN to tell us that a Hare came to watch your lace-making?" asked the neighbours.

"He did indeed, and he was a very intelligent Hare. He called me Queen Anne," said Miss Susan proudly.

"Then he can't have been intelligent, because everyone knows Queen Anne is dead," they scoffed. "You must have dreamed it!"

"You fell asleep and a Hare came past, and all the children ran after him."

"I wasn't asleep," protested Miss Susan. "He asked about lace-making and I showed him how to do it."

NOBODY BELIEVED Miss Susan, but Robin the postman, who was sitting on a spade handle, heard this, and he told Hare.

"We'll hang a piece of lace on Queen Anne's door-knob. Then she can show the village," said Hare.

Grey Rabbit made the most beautiful strip of lace, and Robin the postman hung it on the door-knob of the thatched cottage.

"NOW LOOK!" cried the old lady triumphantly, showing it to her neighbours. "This isn't my work. Did you ever see such lace as this? Grey Rabbit must have made it and Hare told her how to do it and I told Hare."

"We'll put it in the village museum," they said. "It's the strangest lace ever known, and as fine as a fairy's work."

There it lies, in a glass case, with a Queen Elizabeth shilling and a stone arrow-head. People stare at its beauty, and wonder who made it, but we know, don't we?

" SING THE SONG again, Grey Rabbit, the song Hare told you," pleaded Fuzzypeg. " My mother wants to hear it."

" Yes, please sing it, Grey Rabbit," said Mrs. Hedgehog. She wore her night-cap in the day as well as at night, she liked it so much.

So GREY RABBIT sang the little
song and they all joined in the
chorus :
" Queen Anne, Queen Anne, she sat in
the sun,
Making of lace till the day was done.
She made it green, she made it white,
She made it of flowers and sunshine
and light.
She fastened it to a stalk so fine,
She left it in the hedgerow to shine.
Queen Anne's Lace.   Queen Anne's
Lace.
You find it growing all over the
place."

The End of the Story